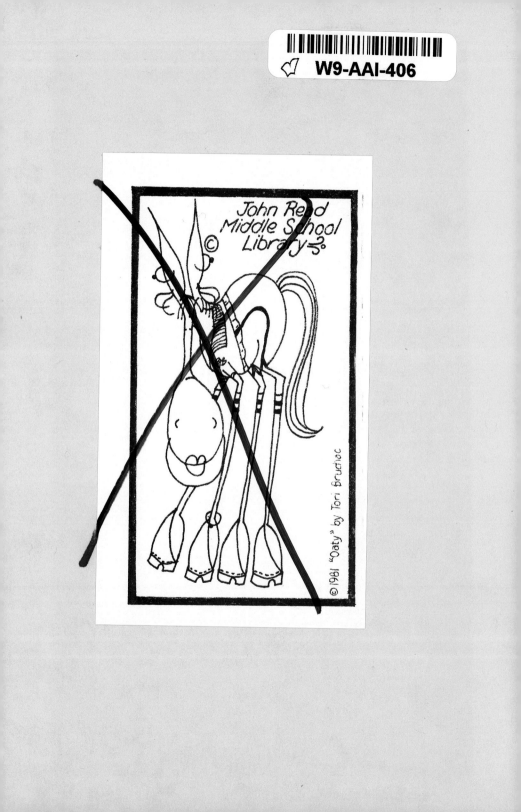

© 1981 "Oaty" by Tori Brudiac

CREATIVE'S CLASSIC STORIES

This short story is taken out of an anthology and presented in its own volume where it stands a better chance of being read and remembered.

In one story, we might see a character survive extreme loneliness, danger, or sadness. Reading about such characters and events can be a powerful experience. And once we've read a good story, it can stay dormant in our memories for years and come to the surface later when we need its wisdom in facing our own danger, loneliness or sadness.

This short story is a well-told classic which has stood the test of time. It is included in Creative's Classic Stories Series and presented with all the dignity and richness a good classic story deserves.

Published by Creative Education, Inc.
123 South Broad Street, Mankato, Minnesota 56001

Copyright ©1986 by Creative Education, Inc. International copyrights
reserved in all countries. No part of this book may be reproduced in any
form without written permission from the publisher.
Printed in the United States.

Cover illustration by Jim Hayes.

Acknowledgement: Copyright ©1971 by Barbara Wersba. Reprinted with
permission from the author.

Library of Congress Cataloging-in-Publication Data

Wersba, Barbara.
  Let Me Fall Before I Fly.

  (Creative's classic short stories)
  Summary: A lonely young boy discovers a tiny circus in his backyard and
its people and activities become all the world to him.
  [1. Loneliness—Fiction. 2. Grief—Fiction. 3. Circus—Fiction] I. Title.
PZ7.W473Le 1986   [Fic]   86-2686
ISBN 0-88682-057-X

LET ME FALL
BEFORE I FLY

BARBARA WERSBA

Creative Education, Inc.
Mankato, Minnesota

When the child first saw them he was not surprised, because it seemed that he had been waiting for them all his life. Rather than shock or amazement he felt only a dim faraway warmth — and it was several minutes before he recognized this warmth as joy. Careful not to alarm them, he lay down on the ground. Above his head the summer day swarmed like bees, like butterflies.

The thing that he had seen was a circus parade, and no member of this parade was more than two inches high. As it passed in front of his face the procession glittered blue and red and gold, and its music was like tiny pieces of glass struck together in the sunlight.

"If I frighten them," thought the child, "they will run away."

But the circus, if it saw a boy-giant lying in the grass, was not afraid. Rolling to a stop at the edge of the lawn, the carved and gilded wagons released their passengers: musicians and clowns, bareback riders and handsome aerialists, dancing girls with feathered plumes, acrobats in pink tights. There were little lumbering elephants and bored-looking camels and Shetland ponies with ribbons in their manes.

Suddenly the child's heart beat quickly because he realized that the tiny circus had come to his house to give a performance...and as though confirming this fact, a whirlwind of activity began. The menagerie tent went up, hauled by the elephants, and the platform for the side show was erected swiftly and expertly. The thin man and the fat lady ironed their costumes while a girl with paper birds in her hair played catch with the midget. Cotton candy booths were appearing, and a faint yet tangible aroma of buttered popcorn filled the air.

"Please," whispered the child, "let it last forever."

And now he realized that he had known these circus people before, known them in some lost dream or vision, and that their arrival was a part of himself in ways he could not explain. He knew that he had been waiting for them since he was very young — and that he must keep them safe and guarded. The thought of grown-ups seeing them made his hands go cold.

The child flattened himself on the grass and watched roustabouts unload wooden poles and spread sawdust in the main ring. Any second, he supposed, the Big Top would go up and the audience arrive. Where would these miniature people come from? Perhaps there were whole cities in the grass which he was unaware of. Perhaps beneath the very ground on which he lay, a network of humming throbbing humanity was preparing to go to the circus — tiny mothers and fathers and even tinier offspring. The child imagined them combing, washing, putting on their best clothes, counting their quarters and dimes. Aware of the mysteries the world held, he shivered with happiness.

Refreshment trailers and ticket wagons were in place along the midway now, and the performers had disappeared. The miniscule roar of lions could be heard — the faintest cracking of whips. The balloon man strolled up and down crying his wares, and the impresario rushed in and out of the stars' tents, chiding, coaxing, encouraging. Above the ground, a complicated web of aerial rigging was being tested. Quite suddenly, twelve "harem girls" appeared in front of the side show and began to dance.

"It's almost time," the child said to himself. "Why don't they raise the Big Top?"

There was a sound of trumpets and into the center ring strode the ringmaster, gorgeously attired in frock coat and boots. After an elaborate bow, he blew a shrill blast on a whistle — and at this signal, the Grand Entry of the performers began. Around the hippodrome they paraded — charioteers and cowboys, acrobats, jugglers and clowns — each keeping time to the martial music of the band and each waving gaily to the audience.

And then the child understood why the canvas had not been raised. The audience was himself.

Once again the ringmaster blew his whistle. But this time, as though a kaleidoscope had burst open, wild activity began in each of the three rings. Bears danced, zebras pranced, horses cantered and leaped. Jugglers juggled silver balls, clowns walked tightropes, two men were shot from a cannon...His heart pounding with excitement, the child watched as Bengal tigers jumped through flaming hoops, as beautiful girls rode elephants, as aerialists swooped through the air like gauzy birds. Each time the ringmaster blew his whistle the acts changed, and one act was more magnificent than another. A seal played the trombone. Twenty clowns emerged from a little car. A smiling llama waltzed.

When the performers took their final bows, the child applauded softly so he would not frighten them. Then, in a moment of inspiration, he picked a rose and showered the tiny people with bits of blossom. The girl with paper birds in her hair bowed very low.

One by one the circus people disappeared into their tents — and the summer day was still. It was as though the performance had never happened, and in the child's heart was a sudden and passionate desire to be small, no more than two inches high, so that he could join them. He sat on the grass until twilight, watching the tents. Pinpricks of light showed through, but there was no sound save an occasional murmur from the animals. The elephants had been watered and stood swaying sleepily. As the first star became visible, the girl with paper birds in her hair stepped outdoors and gazed at the sky. She did not seem to see the boy-giant watching her, and soon it was too dark for either of them to see. With a fall of velvet, night came.

The child could not sleep that night and rose at

dawn, fearful that the circus would be preparing to leave. In his imagination, he saw the tiny people loading their wagons, collapsing their tents, forming a procession in the wan light and marching across the yard. He saw them weaving down the main street of the town and disappearing into the future. If only he were small! If only he could join them and spend the rest of his days traveling from place to place...He ran across the damp grass, but when he reached the edge of the lawn a beautiful sight met his eyes — not a single person had stirred. Only the roustabouts were awake, feeding the animals, and the three wooden rings remained intact. One of the workmen was raking fresh sawdust in the center ring, and it was in this manner that the child understood that the circus had come to stay. This particular circus belonged to him, a gift of fate, and because he was always surprised by happiness, the child wept.

That afternoon the miniature circus gave another performance, and the next day it did the same — but if the performers knew a boy was watching, they did not acknowledge him. It was as if they had decided to remain apart, as if a mingling of the two worlds would be improper. Instinctively the child understood this, and before long he stopped wishing himself small. It was enough to watch the dazzling show that took place every day at two o'clock, and enough to study the entertainers. Each of them had a strong personality, and some were very vain. Peering into their tents, he discovered that the lion tamer spent hours putting on his makeup, and that the acrobats quarreled perpetually about billing. The prettiest bareback rider threw cups and saucers whenever she was criticized — and the ringmaster, doubtless feeling superior to everyone, insisted on dining alone.

By way of contrast, the fat lady, the thin man and the midget were more democratic people who mingled freely with the roustabouts. This happier group spent its evenings playing cards and drinking coffee while the balloon man, festooned with his wares, watched from a high stool. An old clown bored the other clowns by telling the same stories over and over. The youngest aerialist did nothing but practice on the high wire — hoping perhaps, to become a star.

Each of them was different and each was beautiful — but it was the girl with paper birds in her hair who touched the child's heart. Like himself, she was an awkward person who never seemed to do anything right. When she worked with the side show as a "harem girl," she was terribly self-conscious, and when she assisted the juggler she dropped things. She appeared to have no role in the circus except to fill in for people who were sick, and to run errands. The child studied her closely and saw that although she was not pretty there was something original about her. The birds she wore, for example, and her way of holding her head erect when she was unhappy.

Sometimes she would sit with the old clown, listening to his stories, and if they bored her, she did not show it. Sometimes she stood on the edge of the circus grounds watching the evening star — and at these moments the child felt closest to her because he knew what she was thinking. Like himself, she was longing for someone to speak to her who would understand the deep things in her heart. Like himself, she wanted to be loved.

The fact that they could not talk to one another seemed a great misfortune, and there were times when he had to stop himself from touching her, ever so gently. "Even if I held her in my hand," he thought, "I would probably hurt her." And once, when an acrobat fell and broke his leg, and was nursed by the girl, the child felt a sudden jealousy. He could not explain these feelings because he had never had them before — but everything the girl did seemed important and wonderful. Every time she smiled he found himself smiling too.

Dawn. The elephants are watered. Daybreak. A trainer exercises the ponies. Noon. Circus people stroll about in their dressing gowns. At two o'clock the performance will begin...This had become the child's world, and as the days passed he found himself drifting farther and farther away from the life he had known before. His mother spoke to him and he did not hear her. His father scolded, and the child glanced up from his daydreaming with blank eyes. He had always angered them by failing at anything he attempted, and now, as though to stretch their patience to the limit, he was becoming distant, peculiar, vague. What's wrong with you? they demanded. Listen to us! they said. The words fell through the air like raindrops and meant nothing.

If he was peculiar and vague, if he failed at everything, if grown-ups were critical of him, it no longer mattered. He had a friend who wore paper birds in her hair and who did not mind when people laughed at her. It was true that their friendship had never been acknowledged — but the child was beginning to believe that she was communicating with him. Every evening at twilight she walked to the edge of the circus grounds and waited for the evening star — and at these moments he felt included in the ceremony.

It was not that she spoke, or looked at him, but rather that she accepted his presence as though they had known one another for a long time.

With a sense of surprise, the child discovered that he had a passionate longing to make her happy. She was a solitary person who seemed never to have known friendship, yet in some strange way she was strong. Perhaps he could make her a present...perhaps he could weave a tiny necklace of flowers...perhaps he could paint her likeness on a little stone...But nothing was good enough. She was like a princess to whom one is afraid to offer trifles.

The fact that the girl loved the circus people — each and every one of them — made the child love them in ways he did not know he could love anything. Every day they put on their makeup and entertained him, but when the performance was over, they were themselves again — frail and sometimes sad human beings. Did the fat lady have children somewhere in the world? Had the midget ever wanted to be tall? Why did the old clown tell stories about himself that were obviously untrue? The child had never thought about their lives. Now he saw that beneath their glamour, the entertainers held within themselves the weight of disappointments and the ashes of things that had failed.

He had daydreams about the girl. And in his mind they were always the same size and the same age — two people who were so close that they seemed like halves of a coin that had been split apart and then put back together. He imagined that they were playing in a castle of glass, and that they walked through fields of diamond flowers. He imagined that they swam together to the bottom of the sea, and that the sea was made of liquid jade. The daydreams shimmered and sparkled. Paper birds flew through skies of sapphire...

All this time the child had kept the circus people guarded, watching with relief as the rosebushes above the circus grounds grew full and thick. His parents rarely walked in the garden, and it was his job to mow the lawn and tend the few flowers. Never had he been so glad of these chores. Never had he taken care of the garden so meticulously. If a dog or cat strayed across the grass, he frightened it away. If other children looked over the fence, he pretended not to see them. Hearing rain in the middle of the night, he would steal outdoors to plant an umbrella over the little city of tents. He protected the entertainers as though they were his children, and, though he could not have confessed it to them, he took a secret pride in everything they did.

And then his mother said: Tomorrow we go to the seashore.

He had forgotten. She had told him, but he had forgotten — a week's vacation with friends, many miles away. It was too awful, too horrible...He could not go! Suppose somebody found them, suppose a cat came into the yard, suppose it rained, suppose the birds swooped down...He grabbed his mother's arm and implored her. He ran to the garage to find his father. "I can't go! I have things to do here. I'll stay by myself. Please. It isn't important for me to go! Don't you see? *I can't go away.*" He ran back and forth between them like a mad thing, pleading, begging, sobbing. He threatened to hurt himself, to set the house on fire — and finally his father slapped him. As though a balloon had been deflated, all the effort went out of the child and he was silent. How terrible that at each crisis of his life he had to learn the same lesson all over again. The world belonged to them.

That night when it was dark, when a fall of velvet had slipped down over the garden and the evening star hung blue and icy in the sky, the child walked across the lawn. Pinpricks of light showed from inside the circus tents. A tiny tiger growled in its sleep. At the edge of the circus grounds stood the girl with paper birds in her hair — and, as always, she was gazing at the sky. The child lay down on the grass, very close to her, and began to speak.

"I have to go away tomorrow, and there's nothing I can do about it. They won't let me stay here alone. I feel terrible about going because I'm afraid something will happen to you — to everyone — but there's nothing I can do, so please, please don't let anything happen. I'll be back as soon as I can and I'll bring you something from the seashore."

He waited for her to reply, but there was only silence. For a long moment both of them gazed at the star that had been so important in their friendship. Then, as he knew she would, she turned.

The boy-giant and the girl with paper birds in her hair smiled at one another — and their smile was so full of happiness that they did not need words. For the rest of the night he lay close to her, warm despite the damp grass, and it was only when the evening star had grown pale and silvery that he rose to his feet and walked back across the lawn. She waved to him once, and then the sun rose.

At the seashore the weather was gray and windy. Gusts of salt air blew the waves into whitecaps, and enormous gulls sailed overhead. Steamers puffed on the horizon. Trawlers passed — their holds piled high with squirming fish. The child saw none of these things. Head lowered, he walked along the beach, and whenever he saw a tiny seashell he picked it up. He had gathered dozens of them for her — shells in the shape of stars and shells as smooth and black as onyx. There were pink shells and amber shells, and not one of them resembled another. He filled a box with cotton and wrapped each shell carefully, trying to imagine her face when she saw them. For the first time, the child wondered why the girl with paper birds in her hair had joined the circus. Perhaps her parents had been disappointed in her and she had run away...There was no pleasing grown-ups. When you did your best, they were still vaguely disappointed — and when you did your worst, they pretended to stop loving you. How beautiful it would be if he and the girl could live in a land in which no harsh or critical words were spoken.

The circus would continue forever, and the fat lady, the midget and the old clown would be his friends for the rest of his life.

On the last day of vacation, the child sat on the beach and counted boats. It was the only way he knew to make the time pass, and after he had counted fifteen trawlers, thirty sailboats, twelve cabin cruisers and two dozen sailfish, the morning was over and the car was packed and they were heading home. He pressed his face against the car window and tried to stop the pounding of his heart. In his hand was the box of shells, and as he thought of giving them to the girl, his face broke into a grin. He had been foolish to worry about the circus people when long before he knew them, they had traveled through the world without calamity — laughing, quarreling, giving their shows. They had probably spent an uneventful week. The old

clown had probably bored everyone with his tales —
and as surely as night came every evening, the girl with
paper birds in her hair had stood at the edge of the
circus grounds and waited for her star. With a flash of
insight, the child understood what the star meant to
her. It was silvery and cool and remote: a place
without pain.

The first thing he saw as the car pulled into the
driveway was that a tree had fallen in the front yard.
And the second thing he saw was an enormous puddle
of water on the lawn. There must have been a storm
last night, said his mother, a bad storm. It must have
been a northeaster, said his father. The dining room
window is cracked where the tree fell, said his mother.
Could have been worse, said his father. I suppose
so...the yard is soaked...nevertheless...only one tree
down...

Very slowly, as if he were moving in a dream, the child walked around the house and into the back yard. His shoes sank in the wet grass and elm trees dripped moisture on his head. There were puddles of water everywhere, and fallen branches, and a bird's nest — shattered.

Where the circus had been was a pool of mud. Nothing remained — not a tent or an animal or a bit of rigging. Carefully, and without any emotion, the child began to dig in the mud, piling it to one side. He dug until his hands were raw. He dug until the sweat ran down his forehead and blinded his eyes — and when he had dug at least two feet in the ground, he realized that there would never be a trace of them. They had been swept away like so many bits of tinsel, like the spokes of a dandelion wheel, like ashes. Then he saw a tiny yellow object in the grass, and picked it up. Before it disintegrated between his fingers, he realized that it had been a paper bird.

The grown-ups did not understand his silence. They did not understand why he refused to talk or eat, and finally they began to question him. What's wrong with you? Are you sick? Speak to us! Has anything happened? What's *wrong*? Why are you acting this way?

He had lost the desire to live — and at night he lay between the covers with staring eyes. There was no longer anything to be done or to be hoped for. Everything had ended, the way a play ends, and that was that.

They telephoned his grandmother. They scolded and threatened him. They said that he would be punished if he continued to act this way, and that the consequences of his behavior would be serious. They lost their tempers and shouted at him. They took hold of themselves and spoke softly. After a week had passed, he told them.

He did not want to do this, and in the truest and deepest part of himself he knew that he was committing a betrayal. Nevertheless, because they would not let him alone, he said that he had once known a group of circus people who were only two inches high, that they had performed for him every day, and that the storm had killed them. He could not bring himself to mention the girl. He kept her silent in his heart.

His parents thought that he was joking. But when they saw his seriousness and his suffering, when they realized that he wanted to die because his friends had died — then they went very pale and made some phone calls in the other room. Quite suddenly they were kind. His mother held him on her lap. His father stroked his hair.

You didn't see them, darling. They were only a dream.

They were in your imagination. Isn't that right?

They were only a dream, darling. Something in your imagination.

The next day a doctor came to the house, and the child understood at once that the doctor did not wish to examine his body, but his mind. He was asked many questions, and tried to answer them because the doctor was gentle. Some of the questions, however, he could not answer because they had to do with his private world: the part of himself that saw faces in the ocean — the faces of old men with their beards floating above the waves. He could not tell the doctor that he had once heard an invisible child speaking to him, imploring his help, or that he sometimes felt that he had lived in other centuries — a warrior, an actor, a knight. It was impossible to discuss these things with grown-ups.

Perhaps the circus came to you in a dream, said the doctor. Perhaps you had the dream many times, and therefore it seemed real. Many things in our imagination take on the shape of reality. There is nothing wrong with that.

But there was — most obviously — something wrong with it. His parents spoke of him in whispers, and when school started he did not have to go. They bought him too many presents and were falsely cheerful. His grandmother came to visit every weekend, and sometimes she and the doctor walked in the garden, their heads nodding like flowers. Everyone was talking about him, yet no one would tell him anything. It was as though he had a shameful illness...

For the first time in his life, the child felt that his parents required nothing of him — and instead of being a relief, this new situation filled him with fear. They had always been angry and demanding — criticizing each of his failures — but now they had assumed a bewildering patience. Anything he did was all right. Anything he wanted was fine. What was the matter with him? He hated being so special, so different. It made him feel vague to himself, and lost.

Dawn. The elephants are watered. Daybreak. A trainer exercises the ponies. Noon. Circus people stroll about in their dressing gowns. At two o'clock the performance will begin...NO, screamed a new voice inside the child. THEY WERE NEVER THERE.

He moved now with utmost caution, suspicious of people and careful not to hurt himself. After a long time he was permitted to go back to school, and when he improved in his schoolwork he felt an angry pride. He had become more selfish and frequently argued with the other children. His visions of old men with their beards floating above the waves, his longing to live in other centuries, his daydreams — all had submerged. He did not want to think such strange thoughts. He did not want to be thought peculiar. With lightning talent, the child learned to act like everyone else — and everyone believed him.

How easy it was to be like everyone else! You competed for prizes and got into fights and talked about baseball. You committed certain conventional crimes — like stealing — and were approved by your friends. You did things after school in groups, and spent your allowance on candy. That is what children do. This is what he did. And it was very simple, and his parents were pleased.

Not once did he allow himself to dwell upon the circus — and because of this, the doctor said he had "improved." Eventually the doctor stopped coming to the house, and had it not been for the loneliness inside the child, he would have believed that he was well again. The loneliness, however, was like a dull pain, like a toothache, and he could not get rid of it. It weighed him down and brought tears to his eyes when he least expected them. The loneliness would not go away — and so, like a dark flower, it grew.

One night he went to bed and could not sleep. Tossing and turning in the moonlight, he tried to keep thoughts out of his mind. At last he fell asleep, and when the dream about the circus people started, he knew it was a dream.

Once again the child was with them — only this time he was their size and they were not in a garden but at the seashore. The weather was gray and windy, and gusts of salt air blew the waves into whitecaps. Everything looked brilliant against the pale sand. Performers stood poised in each of the three rings.

And they have not died, but are there: the jugglers and acrobats, the smiling llama and the elephants, the tigers and bareback riders and clowns. They are waiting for me in each of the rings, and any minute the ringmaster will blow his whistle. Then the whole world will explode in color and the circus will begin.

They have not died because the shrill note of the whistle has split the air and everyone is performing. They have not died because I am dancing with a bear, and twenty clowns have jumped from a little car. Two men have been catapulted from a cannon. A seal is playing the trombone. And they have not died.

The child dreamed that he was a clown and a

bareback rider — that he made the lions sit up and beg
and that an elephant lifted him high in its trunk.
Then his heart stopped as the girl with paper birds in
her hair walked into the center ring and bowed.

She was dressed in silver leotards and an emerald
cape...and she was beautiful. Not just pretty or nice,
but truly exquisite — as though a magician had passed
his wand over her, heightening and articulating every
feature. She tossed the cape aside and began to climb a
rope-ladder into the rigging. A spotlight followed her
and the drums rolled...and suddenly he was with her,
identically dressed, climbing a ladder on the opposite
side. The spotlight flashed back and forth between
them and the drums grew louder. With a shock, he
saw that there was no net below. The audience
expected them to risk their lives.

As if on cue, the audience arrived: his mother and

father, his grandmother, the doctor, and all the boys from school — and as they sat down they multiplied into fifty mothers and fathers, a hundred grandmothers and innumerable doctors. The boys from school split and multiplied like amoebas until every seat in the circus was full.

The child glanced across the arena and saw that the girl with paper birds in her hair was smiling. Unlike him, she was not afraid. Without understanding what it meant, he whispered to himself, "Let me fall before I fly."

Then the two of them grabbed their trapezes and leapt into space — and he fell. He fell more slowly than he could have believed and his stomach was like a clenched fist. Down and down he fell, while a frightened cry rose from the crowd. With a groan he hit the sawdust, and the crowd was still.

The child gazed around him and realized with a rush of happiness that he was not hurt. Looking up, he saw that the paper birds had left the girl's hair. There were millions of them — and their shapes whirled and spun against the ocean. He raised his arms and the birds swooped down and carried him back to the rigging. Without thinking about it, he grabbed the trapeze and jumped into pure air.

The boy and the girl soared in space like silver eagles, and the air through which they flew was the color of tears, of rainbows and lakes. Images blurred and became sharp again. Salt spray dampened their lips. At the end of the act, the girl left her trapeze, did a triple somersault and caught the boy's ankles at the last minute. It was a great triumph — and flushed and excited, they climbed down into the heat and sawdust of the ring. But the audience had disappeared.

Beyond them the waves were gray as steel, the whitecaps frothy. The paper birds had flown out to sea, and a vast silence had fallen upon the world. Hand in hand, the girl and the boy stood at the edge of the surf, and he knew that they belonged to one another. A castle of glass stood high upon the dunes. Diamond flowers trembled in the light.

One by one, their friends joined them — the fat lady and the midget, the old clown, the balloon man — and when all the performers were assembled, the old clown began to play the flute. Everyone smiled, and soon they were all trooping along the beach together, some dancing, some walking, some with their arms about each other — dozens and dozens of circus people streaming along the gray and endless sand, laughing, talking, being themselves, both image and reality, fact and dream, fiction and longing.

And when the child woke, they were still with him.